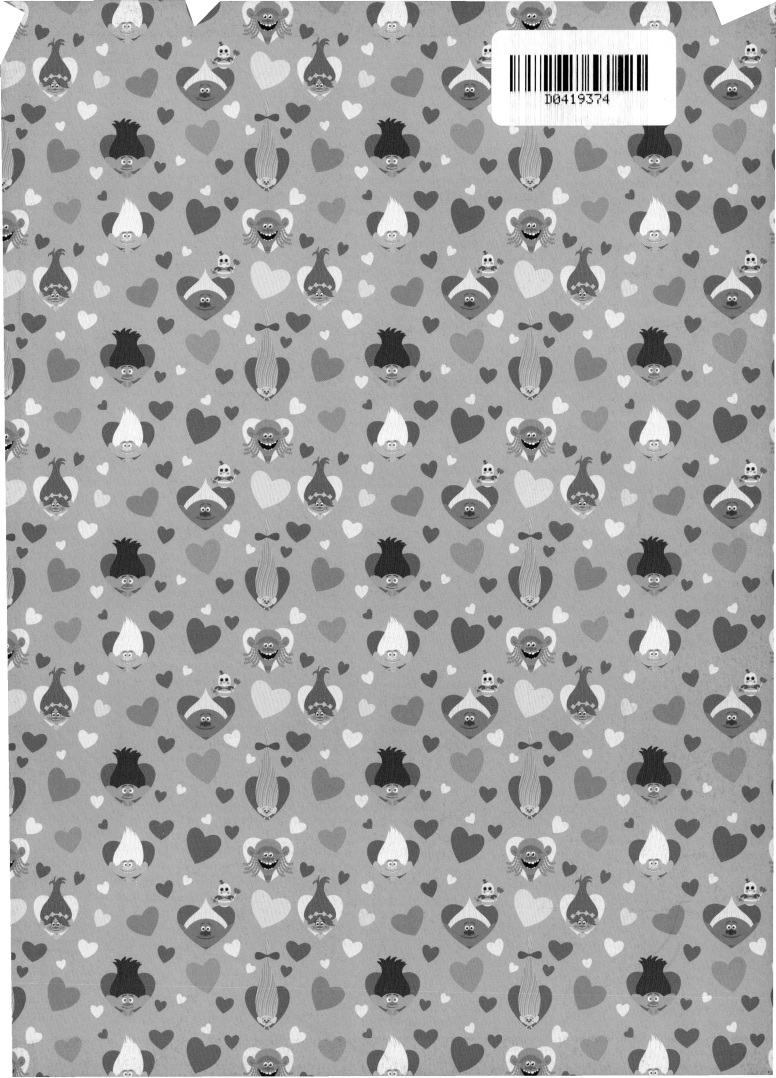

EGMONT

We bring stories to life

DreamWorks Trolls © 2017 DreamWorks Animation LLC.
All Rights Reserved.

Editorial content originated by
Egmont Creative Solutions, London/Warsaw
and Five Mile Press
Cover Art: Karol Kinal
ISBN 978 1 4052 8760 9
67239/3
ID EGM17GLO0447-01

Annual 2018

This Troll-tastic Annual belongs to:

....

Write your name here

CONTENTS

Annual 2018

HISTORY

Once upon a time the unhappy Bergens discovered the super-happy and super-tasty Trolls. They kept them captive to eat on Trollstice ...

... But the Trolls escaped before the Bergen's chef could serve them up for Prince Gristle's first Trollstice feast.

'NO TROLL LEFT BEHIND!'

Twenty years pass, and the day of Poppy's coronation finally arrives. The Trolls celebrate with an extra loud party.

The Bergen ex-Royal Chef overhears the party. Finally, she can get her revenge! She captures some of the Trolls.

Poppy goes to rescue her friends. Branch refuses to help, so Poppy sets out on her own.

Branch changes his mind and catches up with Poppy just in time to save her from a terrible fate. Optimistic Poppy sings all the way to Bergen Town.

'Oh my gah!'

The Trolls befriend Bridget, a shy Bergen scullery maid, and discover she's in love with King Gristle!

The Trolls offer to help Bridget catch the eye of the King. Lady Glittersparkles is born!

To save himself, a Troll called Creek betrays the other Trolls and helps Chef capture the rest of Troll Village. Poppy loses hope and her colour fades away.

Branch sings to Poppy, restoring her positivity and her colours. Branch's true colours return too!

Bridget frees the Trolls. Poppy worries what will happen to her new Bergen friend and turns back to help her.

'Nobody left behind!'

'Hooray!'

The Bergens learn that happiness is found within, not from eating Trolls. Poppy is handed the Torch of Freedom and crowned queen.

Poppy Poppy

Poppy is in high spirits all the time! Read the words below and choose all those that match Poppy and are connected to her nature.

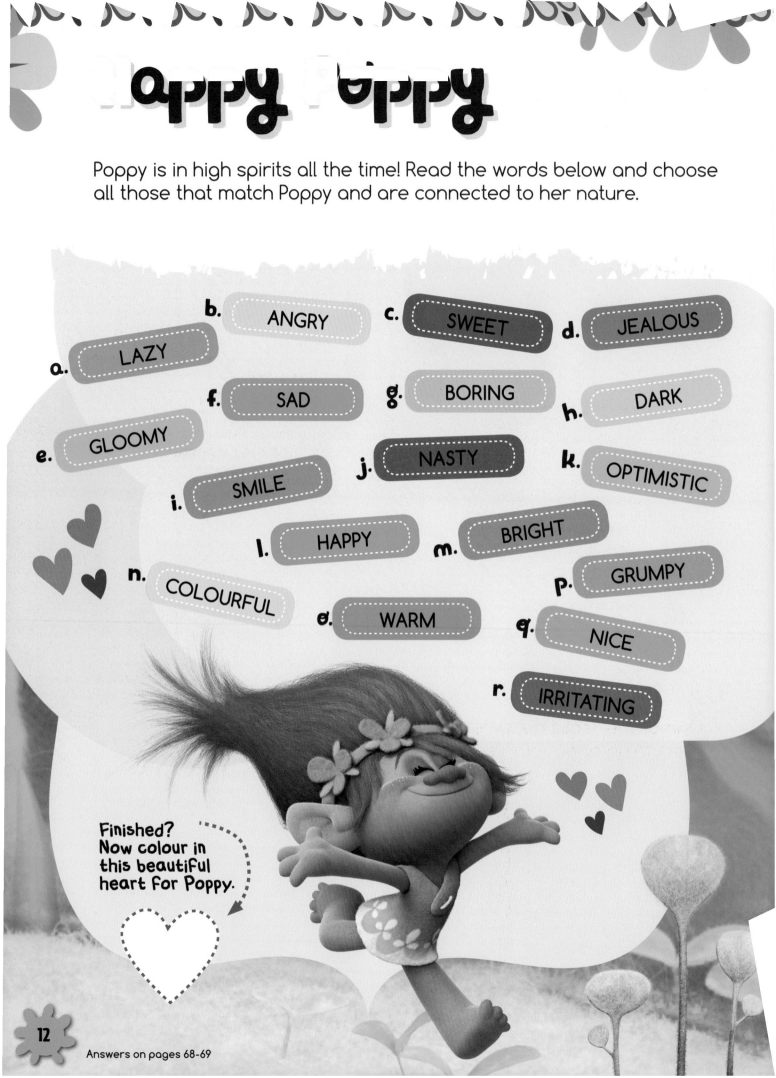

a. LAZY
b. ANGRY
c. SWEET
d. JEALOUS
e. GLOOMY
f. SAD
g. BORING
h. DARK
i. SMILE
j. NASTY
k. OPTIMISTIC
l. HAPPY
m. BRIGHT
n. COLOURFUL
o. WARM
p. GRUMPY
q. NICE
r. IRRITATING

Finished? Now colour in this beautiful heart for Poppy.

Answers on pages 68-69

Magic of nature

Poppy collects flowers and leaves to decorate her scrapbook. Help her solve this sudoku puzzle.

Use the flower code below to fill in the empty circles. Note, each flower type can only appear once in each row and column.

1. 2. 3. 4.

One of the Trolls below is a nature expert and knows everything about plants. Can you guess who she is?

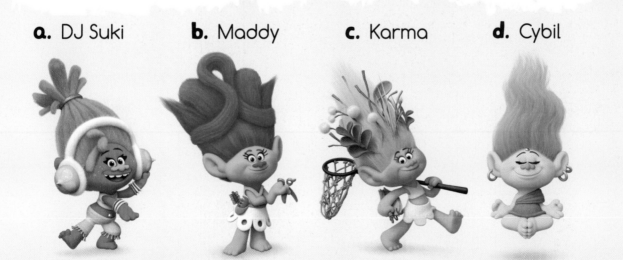

a. DJ Suki   **b.** Maddy   **c.** Karma   **d.** Cybil

Answers on pages 68-69

My friend
BIGGIE AND MR. DINKLES

One's really big and one's really little, but they both love hugs!

He might look all huge and scary, but Biggie's actually just a big softy!

Biggie would do anything to make Mr. Dinkles happy!

You'll always see Biggie wearing his trademark vest and shorts!

We love hanging out and eating cupcakes!

Biggie's not afraid of showing emotions, I often find him crying about pretty sunsets or about Mr. Dinkles' latest hat!

14

Can you spot the 6 things that Biggie changed for the second photo?

Biggie loves dressing up Mr. Dinkles in fun outfits for photoshoots!

Do you know where cupcakes come from?

Mr. Dinkles makes them when he drinks Biggie's happy tears. They are SOOOOO delicious!

Biggie only wants to eat chocolate cupcakes today. How many of them can you spot?

Flower code

Trolls love puzzles. Sometimes Poppy uses a colourful flower code when she wants to say something to her friends. It does sound a fun way to communicate!

Can you help the Trolls solve the puzzle? Write down the letters to read Poppy's message.

Answers on pages 68-69

Who's that?

Hurry! The Bergens are coming!
The Trolls are running for cover –
they hope Chef doesn't spot them.

Can you recognise the Trolls in these close-up pictures? Try to guess and write their names in the frames.

a.

b.

c.

d.

e.

f.

g.

h.

i.

Answers on pages 68-69

Missing friend

Branch spends a lot of time alone, hidden in his bunker. Poppy's going to visit him to show him how beautiful the outside world is.

Help Poppy find the way to Branch by following

this sequence:

START

FINISH

Answers on pages 68-69

Hmazing ornament

Cybil loves mandalas – in her opinion these patterns are full of harmony and happiness. She can find them in the world of nature, especially in flowers.

Colour in the right side to complete this beautiful mandala.

19

Turn to page 44 to see if Poppy finds the baby.

crazy hair

The Trolls' hair helps show their true colours and creates an individual look. Each hairdo is absolutely unique!

Draw lines to join each hairdo to the right Troll.

a.

b.

c.

d.

e.

f.

g.

Branch

Maddy

Harper

Karma

Cybil

Smigde

Guy Diamond

The secret message

Bridget is worlds apart from every other Bergen. That's why Poppy decides to help her get a date with King Gristle. Poppy, the Trolls' Queen, sends Bridget a secret encrypted message about it.

Help Bridget decipher the message. If you find it difficult, use a mirror to read it.

WE WILL DO A NEW FANTASTIC HAIRDO FOR YOU AND HELP YOU CHOOSE THE MOST FASHIONABLE OUTFIT FOR YOUR DATE WITH THE KING.

25

Answers on pages 68-69

Mirror image

Just look at Bridget! She is ready for her date. How do you like her new look and cool rainbow hairdo? She is so excited and can't wait to meet up with King Gristle!

a.

b.

Can you spot which picture matches Bridget?

c.

Sweet baby portrait

Look at this cute baby Troll! Do you recognise whose childhood picture this is? Write the Troll's name in the frame.

Draw over the lines to copy the baby portrait into the grid then colour it in!

. . . .

Answers on pages 68-69

TRØLL VILLAGE

'I love everything about Troll Village. It's completely magical, all neon-bright and sinkably soft and we're tucked away cosy and safe in a sun-splashed clearing deep in the woods. The whole place is so deliciously fuzzy it practically demands petting, from the cheerful, fluffy flowers on the fuzzy ground to our plush, multicoloured felt pods that dangle from tree branches on super-strong strands of Troll hair. Every last inch of Troll Village induces happiness.'

— Harper

You can't possibly get to know the Trolls without stopping for a visit in Troll Village! The problem is that there are so many wonderful things to see and do that you couldn't possibly fit it all in one day. So to help you out we've put together our favourite things to see and do around town.

Before we begin, take a stroll through the heart of Troll Village. All around you are fuzzy and fluffy plants just waiting to be petted! Look up. Can you see all the multicoloured pods hanging in the trees? Those Troll pods are homes, art studios, hair salons, almost anything you can imagine! And the string holding up these wondrous felt creations? Troll hair of course! So hop on your nearest Caterbus and take a ride deep into Troll Village.

1.

1. Poppy's Pod

Where better to start a tour of Troll Village than at the home of the Troll Queen herself? Poppy's pod is party central and Trolls are always receiving handmade invitations to her home.

Top pick as voted by Troll Village

2. Harper's Art Party Pod

This colourful pod is a creative mecca where all Trolls are welcome to express their true colours. If you're lucky you might even have your artwork displayed in Harper's pop-up gallery.

Be careful though! Trolls use their hair as paintbrushes, so paint is always flying across the room. It might not be just your canvas that receives some colour!

2

29

3. Troll Village Cupcakery

The sugar-filled cupcakery is a popular destination in Troll Village. The secret ingredient in the magical recipes? The happy tears of Trolls!

4. Karma's Groovy Garden

Safe and protected within her greenhouse, Karma uses her garden to grow a variety of fruits and vegetables (in case a Troll wants a break from cupcakes). Not only is it filled to the brim with bursts of colour, but the food from Karma's garden is always extra tasty thanks to Troll Village's enchanted soil.

5. A, B, Sing!

This is where all the young Trolls come to learn how to sing and dance. This welcoming pod is the perfect environment for learning how to let your true colours shine!

6. Guy Diamond's Glitterish Grooves

This is Guy Diamond's favourite place to be, besides the Glitter District of course! Fortunately, this pod has a permanent disco ball to keep the dancers sparkling when the Glitter Troll isn't around.

7. Maddy's Hair in the Air Salon

Run by Maddy, the local hair salon guarantees a Troll-do arranged in the most magical of shapes and styles. It's the perfect place to get ready for Poppy's next party.

8. Branch's Survival Bunker

We've saved the most unusual place for last! Unlike any other Troll in Troll Village, Branch built himself a sturdy bunker to live in, complete with a periscope and booby traps. No felt pods for this Troll! This bunker is a must-see location in Troll Village ... that is if you can find its hidden entrance!

FIND YOUR
Inner Troll

Take this test and find out which hair-mazing hero is hiding inside you.

It's party time and you're looking for a new outfit. Do you:

A Get so excited you can't decide what to wear, so ask your friends to help you pick something?

B Decide to go as you are – it'll help you hide in the corner and not talk to anyone unless you really have to?

C Find the most eye-catching, outrageous, super-fun outfit you can? Then cover it in glitter. PARTY ON!

Your friend calls to say she's in a bit of trouble. Do you:

A Drop whatever it is you're doing and give 110% to help however you can?

B Complain about how they've disturbed you, then finally decide to help out, but only a little bit?

C Go completely overboard and act like the world's ending? Then promise to help – as soon as you've done your hair.

Your family is going on a big summer holiday. Do you:

A Get involved in all the planning, listening to everyone and making great suggestions too?

B Ignore what everyone else is doing and come up with your own super-detailed (better) plans?

C Leave the boring stuff to other people and start making music playlists and thinking of awesome travel games to play?

Which pet would you prefer?

A A puppy. Cute, huggable and with bags of energy. Just like you!

B A fish. Quiet, doesn't always look for attention or bother you. Sounds perfect.

C A real show-stopper like a parrot. It's exotic, colourful and eye-catching.

What do you do to relax?

A I love to just hang out with my friends and chat. I like to sing too.

B Relax? Who has time to relax? You never know what's coming so you have to always be prepared!

C I'm always relaxed because life is one big glittery ball of fun to me. Anyone for a party?

What's your favourite kind of music?

A Anything that makes me smile and want to sing along. Happy music!

B I'm not really a music fan, but anything really, as long as it's not too loud.

C If it's got a great beat and I can get up there and strut my stuff, then it's the music for me!

How did you SCORE?

Mostly A:

Your inner Troll is just like **Poppy**.

Always happy, huggable and looking on the bright side, you love your friends and they love you!

Mostly B:

Branch is your inner Troll match.

You may be a bit grumpy at times, but when it really matters you're always there for your friends.

Mostly C:

Oh boy, you're just like **Guy Diamond**.

The life and soul of the party, you're BIG, BOLD and SPARKLY! If your friends are looking for fun, then they look for you.

33

Dinner double

Can you spot 15 differences between these pictures of Chef looking to cook up a treat for Trollstice?

Help Chef create her special Trollstice sauce by choosing the sequence of splashes which adds up to lowest amount.

a   6 7 4 3 5

b   9 6 9 4 5

c   3 3 8 7 2

Did you know?

Chef wears a satchel around her waist especially for holding captured Trolls!

Bridget has hidden Poppy and Branch in a pile of rubbish. Help Chef find the correct pile by working out which one has an **even number** of cups in it.

1

2

3

Answers on pages 68-69

9 1 6 ☐

5 1 3 ☐

1 9 9 ☐

My friend
Cooper

I've never met any Troll like Cooper. He's totally unique! Here are all my favourite things about him.

Cooper's a really special Troll because he has fluffy hair all over him!

Cooper's nearly as musical as DJ Suki. He blows a mean harmonica, I love his wicked solos!

Check out that hair! Cooper's two-toned hair makes him extra magical and cuddly!

If ever I'm feeling down about something I just talk to Cooper. He's crazy positive about everything all the time!

Cooper's cool, unique look is due in part to his trademark green cap. Can you tell who else is wearing it below?

a

b

c

Having four feet means Cooper has dancing skills like you've never seen. I love his funky moves!

Invitiation for celebration

Poppy's coronation is coming soon! She uses her scrapbooking skills to create beautiful, special invitations for her friends. She wants them to match the Trolls' characters!

Match the invitations to the right guests, then write their names on them.

1.

Special invitation for:

....

2.

Special invitation for:

....

3.

Special invitation for:

....

4.

Special invitation for:

....

Karma

Biggie

DJ Suki

Harper

Answers on pages 68–69

The garden mystery

Karma takes care of her garden. She keeps the plants in special order.

Look at these plant sequences. Draw the right flower in the space at the end of each row to complete them.

a.

b.

c.

d.

e.

POP TO PO_PY'S Party Place!

Get a fast beat in your feet and zip around the board to Poppy's pod!

You'll need:
- 1 or 2 dice
- Coins or other counters

1 Roll the dice. Move your counter the number of spaces, following the instructions as you go. Make sure to look out for the special challenges on Poppy's Party Piece spaces!

2 The first player to reach Poppy's party is the winner!

Poppy's party is as happy as HUG TIME!

HOU... PLA...

9 Glitter bomb! Jump to square 19 to join Guy Diamond!

8

7

Poppy's Party Piece:

6 Give every player a hug!

5

4 You've got your bouncy hair on! Bounce to the next square!

3

2

1

START

10 Your party hair is raising the roof! Roll again!

?1 Poppy's Party Piece:

13

29

17 Mud patch alert! You're stuck here for 1 turn!

6

25 Poppy's Party Piece:

40

11 Pretend to eat a cupcake!

12

13 You're a singing superstar! Go forward 2 spaces.

14 Stop to sniff the flower. Miss a go!

32

33

34 Cupcake overload! Miss a turn!

15

37

36 Jump to square 41 for a party makeover!

35

16

17 Too much singing! Sit here for 1 turn.

You did it! Now let's party - Troll style!

FINISH

Yay! Party!

44 Nearly there! Do a crazy happy dance!

39

40 Mr. Dinkles needs a hug! Go back 2 spaces!

18

19

41

43

42 You're spinning some Troll-some tunes! Roll again!

20

Sing your favourite song!

23 Glitter bomb! Jump to say hi to Guy Diamond on square 33!

22

21 Do a Troll-tastic dance move!

What's wrong?

During the party, Poppy's friends prepare a game for her. She has to find one Troll in each row who is different from the rest.

Can you help Poppy solve this puzzle? Look carefully at all the images and spot the odd ones out.

1. a. b. c. d.

2. a. b. c. d.

3. a. b. c. d.

4. a. b. c. d.

42

Answers on pages 68-69

Let's party!

Everything is ready for the party in Troll Village. There are plenty of cupcakes everywhere! Each kind is displayed on a separate plate, but there is something wrong on each one ...

Spot the cupcake on each plate that is different from the rest.

1.
a.
b.
c.
d.
e.

2.
a.
b.
c.
d.
e.

3.
a.
b.
c.
d.
e.

43

Answers on pages 68-69

45

That's HAIR-LARIOUS!

Give your friends a giggle with these super silly jokes.

What kind of flowers grow on your face?

Tulips!

Why was Branch's hair sticky?

How do you wrap up a cloud?

With a rainbow!

Because he used a honeycomb!

What has no fingers, but lots of rings?

A tree!

What makes music on your head?

A head band!

Why did Cooper run around his bed?

To catch up on some sleep!

What's the most musical bone?

A trom-bone!

Say cheese!

Look at this awesome snapshot! It is Poppy's favourite photo with her friends. Unfortunately she dropped it and the picture broke into many pieces!

Help Poppy repair the photo by matching the pieces to the right places in the frame.

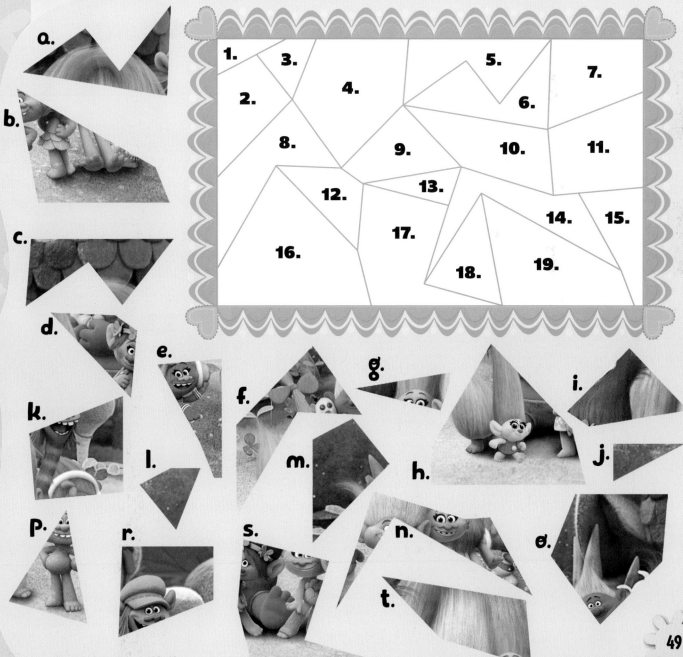

Answers on pages 68-69

True or False?

Think you know everything about Trolls?
Try these tricky true or false questions!

1. Poppy's dad is King Peppy.
TRUE/FALSE

2. Poppy wears red flowers in her hair.
TRUE/FALSE

3. Biggie is one of the smallest Trolls.
TRUE/FALSE

4. Mr. Dinkles makes cupcakes from leaves and twigs.
TRUE/FALSE

5. Cooper is an excellent harmonica player.
TRUE/FALSE

6. Cooper has a twin brother called Dave.
TRUE/FALSE

7. Smidge has a really, really low voice.

TRUE/FALSE

8. Smidge's favourite hobby is hugging trees.

TRUE/FALSE

9. DJ Suki plays critters like musical instruments.

TRUE/FALSE

10. DJ Suki has super strong feet.

TRUE/FALSE

11. Guy Diamond really doesn't like going to parties.

TRUE/FALSE

12. Guy leaves glitter everywhere he goes.

TRUE/FALSE

13. Satin is blue and Chenille is pink.

TRUE/FALSE

14. They're the most fashionable Trolls in Troll Village.

TRUE/FALSE

15. Branch lives in a pink pod.

TRUE/FALSE

16. Branch loves Hug Time!

TRUE/FALSE

FOR TROLL EXPERTS:

This Troll is Poppy's Grandma.

TRUE/FALSE

Answers on pages 68-69

Beat the Bergens!

Are you brighter than a Bergen? Whizz through these puzzles and help the Trolls save the day!

Suspect sauce...

Chef is sorting out her bottles of Trollstice sauce. Put them in order - with the bottle with the **least** sauce in first and the bottle with the **most** sauce in last!

a   b   c   d   e   f   g

Modern art!

King Gristle has ordered a new painting for his room! **Add up** the different shapes in the picture to find out how many **Trolls** Chef needs for her recipe.

green squares		blue rectangles		
+		+	=	

Trolls!

Secret style!

Bridget is choosing hair colours for her make-over into Lady Glittersparkles. **Circle** each word that **doesn't** match it's colour.

Green

Purple

Pink

Orange

Yellow

Blue

Hair-raising escape!

Quick! **Which exit** out of King Gristle's castle can Poppy and Branch use?

A   B

C   D

Tick the exit.

A ☐

B ☐

C ☐

D ☐

You did it! Trolls are off the menu!

Hug the bug

The Trolls are looking for bugs. The forest is full of strange and beautiful creatures. Can you help the Trolls find all of them?

How many bugs of each type can you see in the picture? Count them and write the totals on the lines.

. . . . .

. . . . .

. . . . . .

. . . . .

. . . . . .

What a mess!

The Bergens' world doesn't look as nice and tidy as the Troll Village. Just look at this mess!

Can you clean up all the things below? Match them into identical pairs. Which one doesn't have a pair?

TROLL LIFESTYLE

Now that you've been for a ride around town, it's time to really experience the Troll way of life. It's not all cupcakes and rainbows ... there is also hugging and singing and dancing, and it all comes with a healthy helping of glitter!

1. Hug Time

Drop everything, it's Hug Time! Trolls love to hug. In fact, they love it so much that they made it an hourly event! Every hour, on the hour, a flower blossoms on every Troll's magical Hug Time watch. At that moment they grab those nearest to them and pull them into an epic group hug. The more Trolls the better! After all, who couldn't use a hug?

3. Hair

A Troll's hair does so much more than make a statement about their personality. It also plays a crucial part in a Troll's day-to-day lifestyle. Troll hair is super-strong and the Trolls can stretch and shape their hair instantly into any form you can imagine! Trolls are regularly seen swinging or zip-lining through the trees by their hair, or snoozing in a temporary Troll hair hammock. When it comes to Troll hair, the possibilities are endless!

2. Music

The only things Trolls love more than hugging are singing and dancing. With its sweet acoustics Troll Village is constantly pulsing with music, and it's not unusual for a single song to start off an impromptu all-day dance party!

Music is a very important element of the Troll lifestyle, and opportunities to express themselves in song and dance are never passed up. Even the local critters are known to join in to create some wicked harmonies. As Poppy says: 'With a song in your heart, anything is possible!'

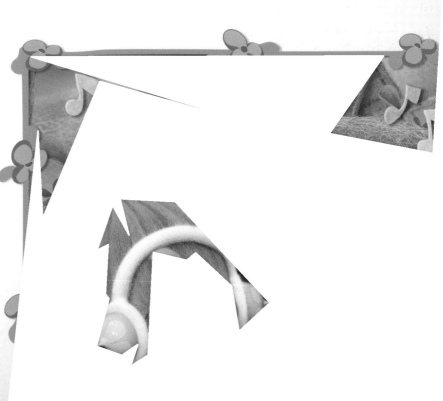

4. Crafting

Satin and Chenille, the fashion twins, are known for their creations. But they're not the only ones who enjoy creating new things. All Trolls love to express themselves with a little (or a lot) of crafting. Troll Village is full of fun colours and textures the Trolls can use when working on their artworks, outfits, scrapbooks ... you name it! Poppy's headband and dress are made of felt and her scrapbook is full of the same fuzzy material (but with a coating of glitter for good measure).

5. Critters

Troll Village is not only filled with the most loving and optimistic creatures that ever existed, but it's also home to a wide array of friendly and huggable critters. From Biggie's pet worm, Mr. Dinkles, to the Caterbuses, the critters of Troll Village are just as much a part of the Trolls' lives as Hug Time! They create tasty treats, form sweet harmonies, help Trolls zoom around the village and some even assist DJ Suki in creating her sick beats!

mixed up photos

Wow! Just look at these strange portraits! DJ Suki is an expert in mixing music, but this time she accidentally mixed some pictures! Are you able to recognise these Trolls?

If you are not sure who's who, unscramble the mixed up names to reveal the answers.

1.

ORECPO

_ _ _ _ _ _

2.

BURTZZEF

_ _ _ _ _ _ _ _

3.

REPHAR

_ _ _ _ _ _

4.

GEMSID

_ _ _ _ _ _

Answers on pages 68-69

making patterns

Satin and Chenille designed a special fabric for Queen Poppy's costume and now they are embroidering beautiful patterns.

Try to copy each shape without removing your pen from the page.

The big day!

Bridget is in a hurry – King Gristle is waiting for her. She hopes to surprise him with her new look!

Help Bridget find the right way through the maze to meet her love!

Tr___!

Follow the trail and answer the questions. See how quickly you can make it to the end, then challenge a friend to do it faster!

START

6. What's the name of Poppy's dad?
a King Troll
b King Peppy

1. What is the name of Biggie's bug buddy?
a Mr. Dinkles
b Mrs. Winkles

2. Whose hair is this?
a Branch's
b Poppy's

5. What's the name of this cheeky Troll?
a Guy Diamond
b Benny Sparkles

3. Which Troll plays the harmonica?
a Cooper
b Smidge

4. Which of these cupcakes is different from the rest?

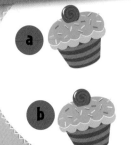
a
b
c
d

SHORTCUT!
Extra hard question!

7. Where do the Trolls live?

a Troll Village

b Troll City

8. Which Troll wears these flowers in her hair?

a DJ Suki

b Poppy

9. Which Troll doesn't like singing?

a Chenille

b Branch

10. Who isn't one of Poppy's Troll friends?

a Bridget

b Branch

11. Which of these critters is different from the rest?

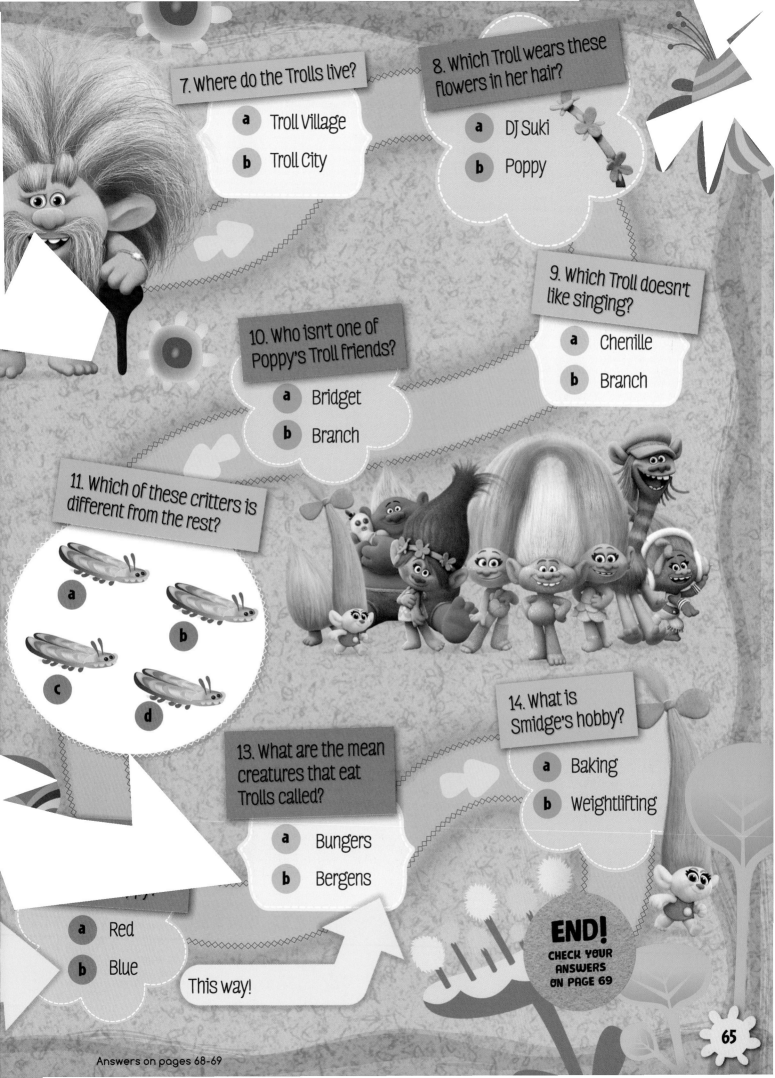

a

b

c

d

14. What is Smidge's hobby?

a Baking

b Weightlifting

13. What are the mean creatures that eat Trolls called?

a Bungers

b Bergens

a Red

b Blue

This way!

END!

CHECK YOUR ANSWERS ON PAGE 69

Let's play together!

Dancing and singing are the two things that Trolls like best of all. Music makes them really happy and it lets their true colours shine!

a.

b.

c.

d.

e.

f.

g.

h.

i.

Look at this cheery scene. Can you spot which of the elements above don't appear in the main picture?

Answers on pages 68-69

Odd one out

When you are a small creature living in the forest it's best to be careful and keep your eyes open at all times. Look at the picture groups below. Everything seems to be fine, but there is an intruder in each row.

Look carefully. Can you spot the odd one out in each row?

1.

2.

3.

4.

5.

Answers on pages 68-69

67

Answers

Page 12: HAPPY POPPY
c, i, k, l, m, n, o, q

Page 13: MAGIC OF NATURE

c – Karma

Pages 14-15: MY FRIEND BIGGIE

3 chocolate cupcakes.

Page 16: FLOWER CODE
NOW IT'S THE HUG TIME!

Page 17: WHO'S THAT?
a – Maddy, b – Fuzzbert, c – Smidge,
d – Cooper, e – Biggie, f – DJ Suki,
g – Poppy, h – Karma, i – Guy Diamond

Page 18: MISSING FRIEND

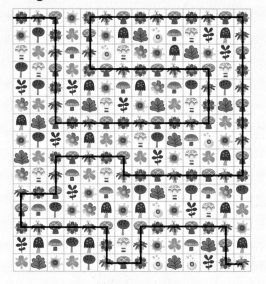

Page 24: CRAZY HAIR
Branch - g, Maddy - a, Harper - b,
Karma - d, Cybil - c, Smidge - e,
Guy Diamond - f

Page 25: THE SECRET MESSAGE
We will do a new fantastic hairdo for you
and help you choose the most fashionable
outfit for your date with the King.

Page 26: MIRROR IMAGE
B is the matching image.

Page 27: SWEET BABY PORTRAIT
It's Poppy.

Pages 34-35: DINNER DOUBLE

Poppy and Branch are in pile 2.
Sequence A is the correct recipe.

Pages 36–37: MY FRIEND COOPER
a – Smidge, b – Creek, c – Fuzzbert

Page 38: INVITATION FOR CELEBRATION
a - Biggie, b - Karma, c - Harper,
d - DJ Suki

Page 39: THE GARDEN MYSTERY
a - 🌸 , b - 🌼 , c - 🔑 , d - 🌼 , e - 🍃

Page 42: WHAT'S WRONG?
1 – d   2 – b   3 – d   4 – c

Page 43: LET'S PARTY!
1 – e   2 – c   3 – a

Page 49: SAY CHEESE!
1-j, 2-m, 3-l, 4-o, 5-c, 6-a, 7-r, 8-f, 9-i, 10-t,
11-k, 12-d, 13-g, 14-n, 15-e, 16-h, 17-s, 18-p, 19-b

Pages 50–51: TRUE OR FALSE?
1. True, 2. False, 3. False, 4. False,
5. True, 6. False, 7. True, 8. False,
9. True, 10. False, 11. False, 12. True,
13. True, 14. True, 15. False, 16. False.
Expert question: False, she's
Branch's Grandma.

Page 52-53: BEAT THE BERGENS!
The sauce bottle order is: e, f, g, c, a, b, d.
Chef needs 21 Trolls (7 + 8 + 6).
Purple and yellow are not correct.
Exit A.

Page 54: HUG THE BUG
🐞 - 5, 🐝 - 4, 🕷 - 3,
🐛 - 2, 🐛 - 1

Page 55: WHAT A MESS!

Page 61: MIXED UP PHOTOS
1 - Cooper, 2 - Fuzzbert, 3 - Harper,
4 - Smidge

Page 63: THE BIG DAY!

Page 64: TROLLS TRIVIA TRAIL
1-a, 2-a, 3-a, 4-c, 5-a, 6-b, 7-a, 8-b,
9-b, 10-a, 11-b, 12-b, 13-b, 14-b.

Page 66: LET'S PLAY TOGETHER!
c, e, h, g

Page 67: ODD ONE OUT
1 –  , 2 – , 3 – , 4 – , 5 –

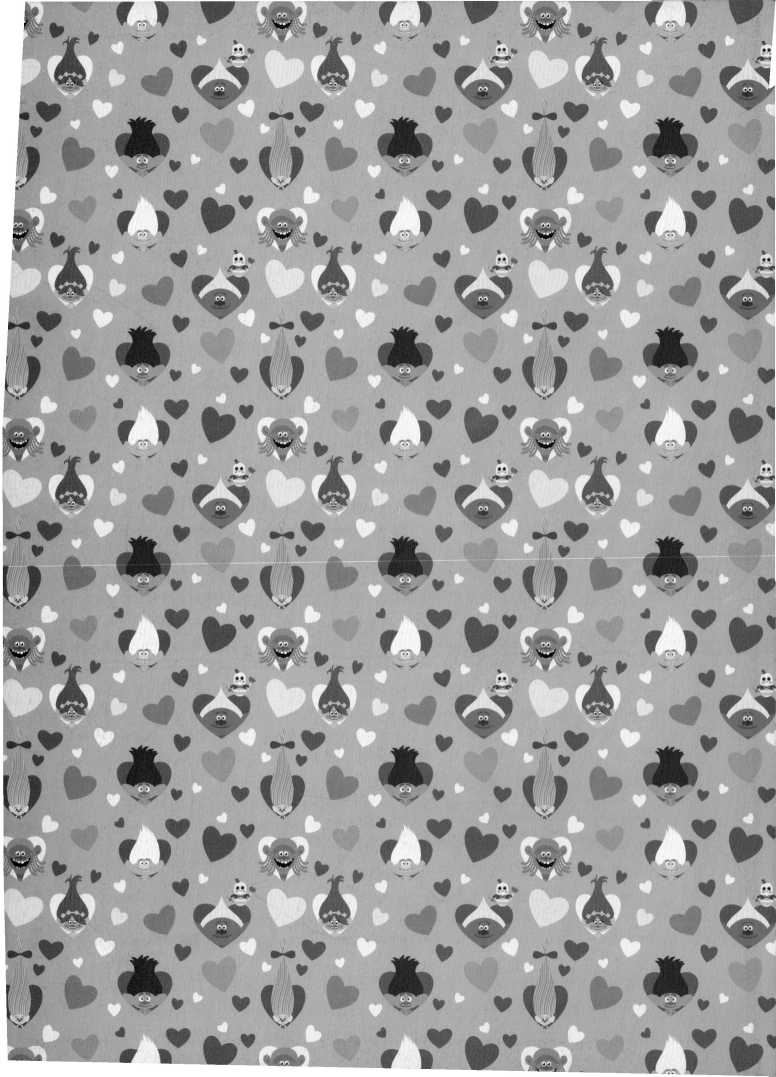